Anthony Palk

The Adventures of Goggle Green
The Arrival

Bumblebee Books
London

BUMBLEBEE PAPERBACK EDITION

Copyright © Anthony Palk 2022

The right of Anthony Palk to be identified as author of
this work has been asserted in accordance with sections 77 and 78 of the
Copyright, Designs and Patents Act 1988.

A CIP catalogue record for this title is
available from the British Library.

ISBN: 978-1-83934-436-7

Bumblebee Books is an imprint of
Olympia Publishers.

First Published in 2022

Bumblebee Books
Tallis House
2 Tallis Street
London
EC4Y 0AB

Printed in Great Britain

www.olympiapublishers.com

Dedication

I dedicate this book to my grandchildren,
Kelsey, Olivia, Tristan and Jack.

CHAPTER ONE

Woosh… a bright flash of green light disturbed the early morning gloom.

What on earth was that? thought a concerned Angela

"Peter, Peter, wake up," she cried as she went into her brother's bedroom. "Look, Peter. Look what is that?"

Peter jumped up from his bed, getting his foot caught in his duvet and crashed to the floor.

"Where is what? What's all the fuss about?"

"Look, here, can you see that thing at the bottom of the garden?"

"Gosh! It's a space ship or something isn't it?" said Peter rubbing his sleepy eyes.

The whole of the garden was glowing with a bright green light.

Peter and Angela live in a cottage in Coggins Mill, a small hamlet just outside Mayfield in Sussex England.

Their bedroom windows overlooked the largest part of the garden at the rear of the cottage.

Their mother and father were still asleep in a much larger bedroom at the front.

"Shall we wake Mum and Dad?" asked Angela.

"No not yet, I think we should wait and see what happens. Hey look at that!" Peter stopped suddenly, his face was agog as he flung his arms around his sister and began to shake.

"I'm frightened too," said Angela, "what's happening, is that door opening? Oh let's call Mummy."

"No wait, there is someone coming out. Look it's a…"

"A what?" said Angela, now shaking more than Peter.

"It's a man… I think!"

Peter and Angela were now fixed to the spot and could not even speak as they watched what looked like a small green coloured man climb down from the spaceship. As the glow of green light fell on the little man, they could see he was waving to them.

"What does he want, why is he waving, can he see us?"

Peter, still frightened answered his sister, with a squeeze.

"It'll be alright he looks quite friendly. Shall we go down and meet him?"

"No", said Angela, "let's get Mummy"

"Oh, come on don't be silly." Peter was now feeling a little sure of himself as he watched the man, who continued to wave and indicated he wanted the children to go and help him.

Peter tugged at his sister's arm. "Come on, lets go." Quickly they ran along the landing, being careful not to wake their parents. Spot, their little black and white dog was standing at the bottom of the stairs, his tail wagging furiously, obviously he hadn't seen whatever it was that had landed in the garden. He perhaps thought he was about to get his morning walk a little early.

"Don't let Spot out," Peter whispered to Angela. "He will be frightened and may run off."

At that moment the whole of the sitting room glowed with a warm green colour. Spot ran under the coffee table and started whimpering. Peter and Angela looked in amazement as the green man tapped on the French windows.

Suddenly the glow vanished and it went rather dark. Spot still hid under the coffee table.

"Please let me in, please let me in, I am your friend."

Peter shouted, "Who are you, what do you want, you won't hurt us will you?"

Spot ran out from under the coffee table and started barking at the shape he could see through the glass.

"Come here, Spot," said Peter as he grabbed him and passed him to Angela. "He'll wake up Mum and Dad, so hold him while I let the man in."

"Are you sure you should? You know we have always been told not to let strangers into the house, Peter."

They could see he was only a very small man, in fact a little smaller than them. That made them feel more comfortable, also he was smiling and had a soft round face without a nose or ears.

"I am really sorry to bother you," he said, "but I have had to land my eco craft and need to find a new part for the engines."

"OK come in," said Angela. "Open the window for him, Peter".

"What's going on down there? Are you both up already?" Their mummy was on her way downstairs.

The little man had climbed through the window.

"Quick hide in this cupboard, we don't want Mummy to see you."

Peter quickly pushed the man into the coal cupboard next to the fireplace.

"Hello, Mum, we were just going to get some cereal from the kitchen."

"Well, it's too early for you to be up, you'll wake your daddy and he doesn't need to get up until 7.30 today as it is Saturday and he will not be going to work."

"OK, Mummy," said Angela, "we're going back up now. Can we take Spot with us?"

"Alright then but keep the noise down, won't you?"

Peter and Angela together with Spot followed their Mummy upstairs.

They waited for their Mummy to go back to bed.

"Let's go back downstairs, Peter. We need to let the man out of the cupboard."

"OK, quietly though."

They opened the cupboard door and there stood the strange little man.

"Hello again," said Peter, holding onto Spot so he would not bark.

"Let's go through to the kitchen because we don't want to disturb Mummy and Daddy," said Angela, as she held out her hand towards the man.

"Thank you," he said taking hold of her hand.

"You feel all soft and…"

"Don't worry I'll explain everything to you but first I must have a drink of water, can you give me that please?"

"Yes," Peter filled a tumbler from the tap and handed it to the man.

"Thank you," he said and Peter and Angela stood in amazement as the water quickly turned green, then white, and clear again.

"How did you do that?" asked Peter.

"Oh, I am just making sure the water is pure and clean," he said as he sat down by the kitchen table. "Sit down with me and I'll explain who I am and where I come from."

Both Peter and Angela sat down close together, still not sure what was happening. Spot, who had seemed unusually calm, jumped onto Angela's lap and was making a noise like a purring cat.

"Well, where shall I begin?" said the little man.

He then began to explain, firstly telling the children his name was 'Goggle Green' and that he lived in another solar system on a planet called Verdant.

At one time many hundreds of years ago Verdant was a

planet very similar to earth but there was a flood, followed by a fire that wiped out nearly all the people that lived there. These disasters where mainly caused by climate change and Goggle explained that the climate was changed by the way the people treated the planet. All that was left were a few trees and plants on the very highest ground.

His family originated from this area of high ground and survived. They, with others, were given the task of rebuilding the planet. There are about a thousand 'Greens', all of whom looked like Goggle Green and they are spending all their time improving the environment of Verdant.

"We have special eco powers and we plant lots of trees and flowers and look after our animals and our seas in fact we now live very much like nature intended," said Goggle Green.

"I was on my way to our sister planet, Swoon, when I noticed my eco craft was losing power. I've not travelled on my own before but I had to get to Swoon as quickly as possible because they have problems they needed me to solve."

"What problems?" asked Peter impatiently.

"Well, some of the children of Swoon are getting ill and we think it is something to do with the water they drink."

"Why do you have to go?" What can you do to help them?" asked Peter.

"Well, I have been given special powers to change the environment to help people survive. This was a power given to all Greens after the big fire."

"What are you going to do now? We can't help you mend your machine because we are only children and then how will you get to Swoon?" Angela was really concerned as she was beginning to like this little man with the soft skin and big eyes.

"We'll find a way," said Peter. "Can you take us to your craft?"

"I thought I told you both to go back to bed," shouted their mother as she was about to enter the kitchen.

"I'll see you later," said Goggle Green and with a flash of green light he was gone.

"What about the space craft?" whispered Peter

"It's gone," answered Angela peering through the kitchen window.

"Oh well it's 7:30 now anyway," said their mum. "Dad is coming down so we can all have breakfast together."

Angela and Peter sat at breakfast just staring at each other. "What's wrong with you two then?" asked Dad. "You must have been up to something as I've never known you both so quiet."

"We uh…"

"Nothing," interrupted Peter hoping that Angela wasn't going to spoil their secret.

"Well today your mother and I are going into town to do some shopping so we have asked Granny to come over and keep an eye on you two, unless you would like to come with us?"

"No… definitely not," cried Peter sounding a little too keen.

"Hmm… sounds fishy to me. Are you sure you two aren't up to some mischief?" said Mum with a broad smile on her face.

After breakfast, Mum and Dad went upstairs to get ready for their shopping trip into town.

CHAPTER TWO

"Peter, I'm going into the garden to see what's happened, are you coming?"

Angela began to walk towards the French doors.

"Look," cried Peter, "Goggle Green is back."

The room again filled with a warm green glow and Goggle Green appeared carrying a large piece of metal.

"I think this is the part that needs repairing," he said, holding it out towards Peter.

Peter was too nervous to touch it in case it was hot.

"Don't worry," said Goggle Green, "it is very safe as we only ever use safe materials on all the things we make."

"I don't think I can help you," Peter said, as he was still unsure.

"What about the man at the garage?" suggested Angela.

She remembered her dad had often taken things such as lawn mowers and hoovers as well as his car to Mr. Gregory who ran the village garage.

Just at that moment the door swung open.

"Hello, you two what are you up to?" said Granny.

"We um…" Peter looked around and saw that their friend from space had vanished.

"OK, you two," said Mum, "now that Granny has arrived, we are off to town. Be good and don't give Granny any trouble."

Granny then went into the kitchen. With a flash Goggle Green was back.

"We need to go to the garage," said Angela

"What about you, we can't take you with us can we?" said Peter looking at Goggle Green

"We have to," said Angela knowing that neither of them could explain what the part was, what was wrong with it and even more difficult where it came from.

"I know," said Peter, "why don't we get Mr. Gregory to come to the house?"

"What about Granny?" whispered Angela into Peters ear. "We don't want Granny to see Goggle Green, she will be terrified."

Peter was quick to think up a scheme but still wasn't sure if he could carry it off.

"Oh, we are just thinking of walking to the village if that's all right with you, Granny, as we need to pick up a part for Daddy's lawn mower from Mr. Gregory."

"Very well," said Granny, "but make sure you are both back in time for lunch. I have brought some of your favourite sausage rolls and cream cakes." She picked up Spot and headed back into the kitchen.

It was now a bright sunny morning as Peter and Angela hurried out of the house and began to climb the hill towards the village.

"Peter, we haven't got the part with us and what are we going to tell Mr. Gregory anyway?"

Then there was a flash that stopped Angela mid-sentence.

"Hello again its me." Goggle Green had appeared again carrying the broken part for his eco craft. "Sorry if I startled you," he said. "Can I come with you and explain what I need?"

"No, I think it would be better if we went alone but you need to explain what needs to be done."

"Let's go into this field," said Angela.

They climbed the stile and sat behind the bushes so no one could see them. The grass had a brownish burnt look about it and the sheep looked unhappy with no fresh grass to eat.

"Well, now I will explain how you can help me," said Goggle Green sitting on what looked like an ant hill.

"Be careful," said Peter, "you will get covered in ants and they can bite"

"They won't affect me," said Goggle Green and he began to explain what they had to do. "This piece of metal has a crack in it and in order to repair my eco craft I need to fill the crack with a similar metal and then fit it. The problem is, can we get a similar metal from your friend at the garage?"

"Well, we will have to show it to him," said Angela.

"What about you?" asked Peter.

"I'll wait here until you return. And while I'm waiting, I will make the grass in this field fresh and green so the sheep can enjoy it."

"How will you do that?" asked Angela.

"I'll show you when you return," replied Goggle Green.

So off they hurried. Peter holding the strange piece of metal and Angela getting very excited about how he was going to make the grass greener.

There was no one to be seen at the garage

"Is anyone there?" shouted Peter

There was still no reply.

"Let's go inside," said Angela eager to get things moving. They tiptoed into the workshop being careful not to disturb any engine parts that covered the floor. Then they suddenly they saw two legs sticking out from under one of the cars.

"Is that you, Mr. Gregory?" said Peter tugging at his trouser leg. He didn't move. "Mr. Gregory, are you, all right?" asked Peter

There was still no movement

"Quick, we must get someone," said Angela

Then in a green flash Goggle Green appeared.

"Let me look at him," he asked, and bent down under the old car and pulled Mr. Gregory out.

"Is he… is he dead?" said Angela beginning to shake.

"I think he is," said Peter

"Wait," said Goggle Green and with that he put his hand on Mr. Gregory's head. He turned a bright green then went white and then back to normal.

Another flash and Goggle Green was gone.

"Ah, good morning, you two," said Mr. Gregory. "What can I do for you on this fine morning?"

Both Peter and Angela couldn't believe their eyes, it was as if nothing had happened.

"We have a problem, Mr Gregory," said Peter. "We need to get this piece of metal fixed. It's from Dad's lawn mower." Keeping up the story he had told Granny.

"Well let me see. Gosh, I don't think I have ever seen

metal like this before. You say it's from a lawn mower? Well, it's not one I have ever sold or repaired. Still let's have a look, I've got a special filler that might do the trick."

With that Mr. Gregory went to his tool cupboard and brought out a can.

"We can try this," he said with some confidence.

As he was starting to fill the crack both Peter and Angela wondered what might happen. Then as if by magic the piece of metal began to glow but this time a bright yellow. 'Was this something to do with the filler,' thought Peter. It turned green and then back to its metal colour.

"Well, I'll be," said Mr. Gregory, "you say this was from a lawn mower? Well I'll be, anyway it seems to have done the trick. You can't even see the crack now." Tell your dad I would like to see his lawn mower sometime."

"Thanks, Mr. Gregory," said Peter as he grabbed Angela by the arm. "Come on, let's get back quickly to find Goggle Green."

CHAPTER THREE

They hurried back down the hill careful not to drop the shiny new piece of metal.

"Look, Peter," cried Angela, "the field is so very, very green."

They climbed the stile and couldn't believe their eyes. The field was bright green and the grass had grown at least four inches. This was amazing! Nearly all the fields around were browned by the sun of the long hot summer.

"Over here, Angela," Peter was heading towards a group of sheep who were skipping and seeming extremely happy. "Goggle is over here."

"We've got it fixed," said Angela, "now tell us how you do all these amazing things."

"Well, you can see I carry a lot of equipment," he explained as he touched various items around his person.

"This strap on my arm is my flora and fauna translator, with this I can talk to nature, look I'll show you."

Peter and Angela watched in amazement as he touched a button and a herd of sheep came running towards them. "Wow, that is brilliant. Show us some more." Peter was really excited. "What is that on your belt?" he asked with his face beaming.

"Well, this is what I changed the grass with, it's my eco belt. When I touch this button and programme in what I need to happen, I can alter a lot of the immediate environment."

"What about Mr. Gregory? How did you bring him back to life? Tell us please Goggle," Angela asked impatiently.

"Well actually, he was only asleep." Peter and Angela fell about laughing and remained extremely excited about their latest adventure.

"What are we going to do now? Do you have to go? Can we come with you?" Angela asked.

"Steady on, you two. I have to go back to my craft to see if the fixed part will work. Then we can decide what to do next."

With that they all started off down to Peter and Angela's cottage. "I'll meet you there," said Goggle Green and in a flash, he was gone.

Peter tried to convince Angela that they should go with Goggle Green if they could be sure to be back before their mum and dad returned.

"But Granny wants us back for lunch, and anyhow, we don't know how far he will be going. I am a bit scared, don't you think we should tell Daddy about it?"

"Don't know," said Peter. "Lets just see what happens when we get home."

"Hello, lunch is ready." Granny was standing at the gate. "I thought you were taking a rather long time. Where is that part for your daddy's lawn mower?" she asked noticing they weren't carrying anything.

Quick as ever, Peter replied, "Oh it wasn't ready so we may have to go back after lunch." He was already scheming to be out all afternoon if they decided to go somewhere with Goggle Green.

"Yum those cream cakes were wonderful," said Angela as both her and Peter finished their lunch as quickly as possible, without taking their eyes off the window to the garden. "Why hasn't he come back, Peter?" whispered Angela so Granny couldn't hear.

"I don't know," answered Peter. "We are going out to play in the garden if that's OK," said Peter and he grabbed Angela's hand. "Come on, let's go."

"Wait a minute," said Granny, "I've got a small chore for you to do."

Angela and Peter looked at each other wondering what Granny may want them to do and how it might interfere with their plans.

"Mrs Kay, who lives in one of those pretty little cottages at the end of the village, has a problem with her garden. All of her flowers and grass are dying because of this hot summer. So, I said I would send you along to water everything."

"OK, we would love to," said Peter hoping he could get it done quickly enough to not interfere with their plans with Goggle Green. "We'll just go into the garden for a short while, and collect up the watering can and hose," suggested Peter, hoping this would give them a chance to find Goggle Green.

"Alright, Peter, but let me know when you are both leaving and I will ring Mrs Kay to say you are on your way," said Granny a she cleared away the lunch.

CHAPTER FOUR

"Where is he? I can't see the eco craft. Has he gone already?" Angela was getting frantic "Surely he would have said goodbye!" she exclaimed.

Then suddenly, just as before, a green haze appeared to cover the whole garden. There before their eyes was the eco craft.

"It obviously worked then," said Peter, assuming Goggle Green had used the fixed part.

The light became normal and a door on the top of the craft opened.

"Hello, it's all fixed, thank you very much. I must go to Swoon now as there is work to do."

"How long will it take? Will we back in time for tea?"

"Hold on," said Goggle. "I can't just go like that with you two on board. I could be gone for at least a year."

"A year," cried Angela realising that their adventure was about to end.

Suddenly a light started flashing on the side of the craft.

"Wait there," said Goggle, "it's my envirophone."

He went inside the craft. Peter and Angela waited and discussed what they could do to keep Google Green around a little longer.

"Well, I have to go to a place called Scotland" said Google as he emerged from his craft.

"There has been an oil spill off their coast from a tanker and it's likely to create a slick along a large portion of the coast."

"We'll come with you, it's not far," said Peter.

"Of course, it is," argued Angela, "it's about eight hundred miles.

"Goggle, how long would that take?" Peter was hopeful Goggle would say not long.

"About twenty minutes, I should think if you can show me exactly where it is on the universal map." Goggle beckoned them inside the eco craft.

Inside the craft both Peter and Angela stood in amazement at all of the screens, like hundreds of TVs with dials and buttons.

"This is fantastic, where's the map, I'll show you where Scotland is." Peter followed Goggle Green across the big room. The craft seemed so much bigger once they were inside.

"Come over here, Angela, and help. You know about places, don't you?" cried Peter.

The three of them stood looking at a large screen. Goggle pressed some buttons and the planets flashed across the screen.

"It will stop when we see Earth," said Goggle, "then we will close in on the land mass and you can show me where Scotland is."

"There," Peter pointed as Earth appeared on the screen.

Goggle pressed some buttons and entered the word Scotland on a keyboard. The picture then showed the British Isles and Angela ran up to the screen and said, "There it is, that's Scotland."

Goggle then took some numbers from the screen and put some more information into his keyboard.

"OK we are ready to go," he said.

The door closed and Goggle asked Peter to take Angela over to the big red double seat with some safety belts.

"Sit there and put on your safety belts," Goggle then went towards his flight deck.

There was a green flash.

"We are on our way now, sit tight for take-off."

"Peter, Peter," cried Angela, "we've forgotten about Mrs Kay!"

"Who is Mrs Kay?" asked Goggle Green.

"Oh, we were supposed to go and water Mrs Kay's garden because all of her plants were dying," said Peter not wishing to halt the start of this great adventure.

"Tell me where I can find Mrs Kay's garden, Peter, and we will do that before we go." Goggle stopped the engines of the eco craft.

"She lives at the top of the village in a little black and white cottage called 'April Blooms'."

Peter was hoping he wouldn't have to get out of the craft.

"Wait here, I'll see to it," said Goggle and with a flash he was gone.

Minutes later he returned. "OK that's dealt with," explained Goggle as he appeared again at the flight deck.

"Let's get started."

CHAPTER FIVE

The telephone rang and disturbed Granny who was snoozing in the afternoon sun as it fell across her big chair by the fireplace.

"Hello, it's Mrs. Kay here, I just wanted to thank you and those two wonderful grandchildren of yours. My garden looks wonderful, I can't imagine what they used in the water. The grass is greener than I've ever seen it and the colours of my flowers are truly beautiful."

"Well, that's fine. I'll tell them you are pleased. Goodbye for now."

Granny was a little annoyed that Peter and Angela hadn't told her they were going to Mrs. Kay's as she had specifically asked them to tell her when they left.

Still at least Mrs. Kay was satisfied, she thought, as she settled back in her chair.

"Look we are above the stricken tanker," cried Peter as he peered into the screen just above their seat.

"Wow that was quick. What are you going to do now, Goggle?"

"Well now I will have to manage the situation on my computer to see how much oil has been spilt," said Goggle as he pushed a few buttons.

"OK, I think I can contain the slick and stop it spreading. That will help protect the birds and fish in the surrounding area."

"Gosh," said Peter, "that will be amazing."

With that a glow of green appeared above the oil slick and the slick started to shrink.

"Can we go home now?" said Angela fearing that they would not get back before their mum and dad arrived home from their shopping trip.

"Just a little tweak and the problem is solved," said Goggle again twisting one of the knobs on his computer. "There that's done," said a happy Goggle as he watched the slick slowly vanish. "You see children, this is just one of the problems that's created by the need for oil to manage things on your planet. Unfortunately, I alone cannot change everything on your planet. There are many things that I can teach you about improving your environment such as not needing to use unsustainable products and therefore reducing waste. These things and more advice I can give you will help you save your planet from the fate similar to that which we experienced on Verdant. However, we don't have time for that now as you have to return home and I must go to Swoon to help with their situation."

Goggle wished he had more time with the children but promised to visit them again very soon.

The journey back home was very fast. Angela and Peter

left the eco craft and waved goodbye to Goggle. There was a flash and the craft and Goggle were gone.

"Wow, how exciting was that?" cried Peter as he chased Angela up the garden path.

"Shall we tell Mummy and Daddy?" asked Angela. "I'm not sure they will believe us anyway and perhaps we should keep it as our secret until the next time."

"Yes, I agree," said Peter. "Let's hope Goggle Green comes back again and we can find out more about learning to improve our environment and save our planet."

With that, the pair entered their cottage with smug smiles on their faces and a certain amount of excitement as to what may follow on another adventure with Goggle Green.

About the Author

Following a career in marketing and brand development Anthony co-produced a fifty-two part television series called Cubeez. The series is an animation aimed at preschool children. Originally aired in the UK it was then shown in over twenty countries worldwide. Available now on YouTube.

Acknowledgements

Thank you to my wife, Maggie, and close friend, Geoff, for their encouragement and help in creating this book.

Printed in Great Britain
by Amazon